The Third Reality – Are we alone in the Universe

By

Jagdish Krishanlal Arora

techbagg@outlook.com

2 Are we alone in the Universe

3 Are we alone in the Universe

Chapters

Introduction

Our Solar System

The Galaxies

The Universe

First, second, third and fourth Dimensions

The Lord of the Universe - God

Time, Space, Matter and Energy

Inter dimensional travel - The cycle of life and death

The Sun as a God and the Creator

Type 7 Planets which have Life in them

Environment on Mars

The Elements of Life and how it got created on Earth

The Earth and its seasons

The Nature of life and living organisms

4 Are we alone in the Universe

The Journey of Life on Earth

Harappa and Mohenjo-Daro and other ancient civilizations like the Atlantis

The Bermuda triangle and Atlantis and the Aryans

Our consciousness and the gravitational pull on the planets in the solar system.

The 5000-year cycle of Time

The Environment on Earth

Our origin on Earth

5   Are we alone in the Universe

Introduction

The book is only for reading and to improve our knowledge of ourselves, the mankind, the Universe, galaxies and stars.

Even with the James Web Telescope, Hubble Telescope, unlimited space missions our knowledge of the Universe, galaxies and stars will always be limited for maybe another few hundred years or more. Maybe, life may end and reactivate like it happened in the past when entire populations and civilizations ended on Earth and started fresh many times.

The information has to be written at once it comes in the mind. If the book is not written then immediately as the information comes, it is impossible to write or complete the book. The information comes from nowhere just like magic. Book can be written only once as it has a large amount of information about our entire Universe in a concise and summarized manner and it is very difficult to write unless information is obtained from nowhere just like the Big Bang Theory which says life came out of nowhere and Universe came out of nowhere.

I myself don't know where the information I write comes from and it is just like creation of planets, galaxies, stars and planets. But as science advances my information will be validated and studied as science in books and colleges similar to what Artificial Intelligence is doing to lives of the humans and animals.

James Web Telescope and Hubble Telescope are showing new things from space which are still mysteries. What the James Web Telescope is showing was written by me around four to five years back. The book I had written was the Journey of Mankind from Earth to Mars and the photos I showed were the same now what the James Web Telescope is showing. The photos of James Web Telescope are not known and they existed before. But it will take time to prove if they are real or not as the images are generated from thousands of individual images.

It will take unlimited number of years to take actual real-life images of stars and

7 Are we alone in the Universe

planets as our cameras and telescopes are not of the required quality and stand to take photos of distant stars, planets and galaxies or any other part of the Universe. Therefore, we have to depend on infrared images made by James Web Telescope and Hubble Telescope which use infrared imaging to make the images of how stars and galaxies look like depending on the light which they harvest from far away objects and convert them into possible images.

My books are sometimes ahead of time, but as time passes by you will see what I write is actually happening or we can now see the third reality with the advancement of science.

To study about the environment of Mars and whether it is suitable for us to live or not, we first have to study our own planet, our solar system, the galaxy we live in and our universe and a little about God.

Mankind has now existed for some thousands of years as per known history. We have not yet known four origins in these few thousands of years, and carbon dating of fossils has given us no information of our origins like they did give information of dinosaurs'.

We have studied a lot about dinosaurs and many movies show us these animals also coming back to life which is not possible as they can be done only in movies and not in real.

Those who know history, also know even after numerous experiments we have not learned about our origins and no evidence has been found about our making either on the planet we call Earth or on other planets in our own solar system.

What I know and what I do not know will be evident to you as you read my entire book. You will not be disappointment as what you will get from reading my book, you will not get in many hundreds of books in one place.

Also, what I will be writing, is also only a fraction of what I know, and everything I know cannot be put into books, because the subject is vast. I have put as much information possible in an easy-to-understand way for everyone to read.

9 Are we alone in the Universe

What you may have seen in a hundred different movies may be here in one place and also information of hundreds of texts and books also, you can find here at one single location.

But here I cannot put figures and calculations, although I know everything, as my book will not complete if I do and to do in-depth studies, you have to refer text books which give deep information.

Our Solar System

Why do we call our planetary system as a solar system. It is because our planets depend on the energy of the Sun to survive and when our sun ends, so do all the planets in the solar system. When we harness the energy of the sun, we call this as solar energy and the instruments we use, we also call them solar systems.

It means al the planets in the solar system run on the energy supplied by the sun. Without that energy, the planets will not rotate either around the sun or around themselves. You know nothing moves without energy or heat supplied to it, so how can planets and their satellites rotate without an energy source.

This requirement of energy for rotation may not be agreeable by scientists as it has never been discussed or even imagined till date. Why I say energy is required, for rotating planets is because science has some theory of spherical objects called inertia, designated by a and b, and there is a formula for two rotating spheres they say there exists kinetic energy between them.

It is surprising that our solar system does not have a name. We have a name for our galaxy, but we have no name for our solar system, and it is just called a solar system.

While the Sanskrit texts mention Navgraha, meaning nine planets system, they include the moon as a planet and also the sun is considered a planet. There are two imaginary planets of Rahu and Ketu also. The Hindu texts and the nine planets mentioned in them do not match with the planet system of ours as we know today.

Only Sanskrit texts mention planetary systems, while other religion texts mention far away stars and civilizations from other stars from where they originate.

The Greek representations of the stars are matching to the stars position we have today also. Whenever any civilization has developed, they have spent a lot of money exploring space and spent a major portion of the taxes they collected on research.

Today also, it is the same situation as governments collect more taxes, they spend more on exploring empty space, and the limit to spend is endless. It is a big space, empty everywhere and to explore it in entirely, it will require spending money for thousands of years. The amount of space we have is very vast, and billions and trillions of dollars are not sufficient to know everything.

You can make thousands and thousands of space crafts, and there is huge space out there and it will take a very long time to explore space.

In prehistoric times, the Solar system was assumed to be flat. It meant that Earth was not a circular body but a flat land mass separated by the rivers, seas and oceans.

13 Are we alone in the Universe

There was no rotation of the Earth, which the earlier humans believed.

Even, I believed the ancient humans for a certain period of time that the Earth was flat, till I investigated fully and studied that rotation indeed existed in al planets including the moons.

Just imagine today people are now able to view the entire Solar system, known as the from our own eyes. We can now see the rotation of all the planets around the Sun in a definite manner. This elliptical rotation is said to have been continuing since the last thousands of years.

Our solar system, is said to be having nine planets orbiting around the sun in the following order from first to last:

Mercury

Venus

Earth

Mars

Jupiter

Saturn

Uranus

Neptune

Pluto

Out of these nine planets in our solar system, only Earth seems to have life. Four out of the nine planets appear to have solid surfaces, which include Mercury, Venus, Earth and Mars.

This is because they have a thin or a transparent atmosphere allowing space explorers to see their solid surfaces.

The outer planets Jupiter, Saturn, Uranus, and Neptune are called gas giants as their atmosphere is supposed to consists of gas and the interior surface is believed to be of liquid metal.

Although, I do not believe in this as for every planet to exist it is supposed to have a solid surface although the inner surface can be of liquid metal or liquid rock.

Pluto was discovered only around the year 1930, so very little is known about it. Sometimes it is considered a planet, and sometimes it is not. Normally, the more the planet is further away from the Sun, the larger it is, but it does not seem to be the case for Pluto.

The four giant planets may be gas giants but cannot have liquid metal rock, as they are very much far away from the Sun to maintain those liquid metal temperatures, unless they have nuclear reactions like the Sun.

Defying the scientific theories, I believe all planets including the gas giants of Jupiter, Saturn, Neptune and Uranus have solid surfaces. These giant planets still can have gases like helium and argon in their atmosphere as well as carbon dioxide, and there are regular volcanic activities in their solid surfaces and in the core.

The last exploration of Saturn was by Cassini, and in its last orbit, the spacecraft plunged into the atmosphere of the Saturn, after that nothing was known of the surface of Saturn.

The first four planets near to the Sun seem to have carbon dioxide due to the fact that the atmosphere permits it to exist and because of the inherent gravity of the planets not because of the temperature although temperatures also have a role to play in it.

The places where I have lived from where I was a small child, had very less access to outside information, but since the year 1980, I got access to every information as it happened, starting from small meteorites hitting the earth, foreign bodies coming to earth every hundreds of years, the first space exploration, shuttle failures, all information was received as it happened.

I have studied all of the Voyager spacecraft missions as well as other spacecraft missions that have explored space, and the results which they have got is only the known planets as we have known, since the ancient times as is there is some books of the ancient civilizations. Other than the known planets, the space missions have found no new planets and no new life on other planets or other solar systems with habitats.

The telescopes installed by humans in space can see the stars, but these telescopes cannot see solar systems like our near us. The Hubble space telescope is the most famous sending very rare pictures of the stars.

This all things are predetermined by God, the information we are supposed to receive, it comes to us, even if we do not have the facilities in the places we live. So that is how we get to know more than the scientists, who discover the things.

The reason we keep the solar systems, apart by a very huge distance is that there is a gravitational pull to these objects. The gravitational pull comes due to the magnetic fields, that we have in these objects. We also have opposite fields, where like objects are supposed to repel each other. Like every planet has a gravitational field, the solar systems also have huge gravitational fields, and they need to be separated by huge distances, so their gravitational fields do not attract each other.

That is why in magnetism we have two types of polarity, one is when two magnets attract each other, and in the other, the magnets repel each other. When a north pole faces another north pole, it repels it and opposite poles attract each other. The proof that each pole of a planet has magnetic energy is proved by the magnetic compass which always points to the north pole.

For different planets, we give different magnetic field strengths to maintain balance between the planets and the solar system. This study is vast, and I will only explain them briefly. This is complex mathematics, how it is done and how planets are oriented in their orbits.

Some more interesting information I will give in my chapter of the Earth, how earth floats in space, the orientation of its axis, rotation and things like that. I know to some people a lot of questions come into their minds, but it is not possible to answer all of those and we must rely on our own consciousness to answer that.

You may not believe, but most of the answers we need are already present in our mind and consciousness and we only have to learn to harness them. We have a connection to our central database which stores all the information our mind has and lots more than that. I do not keep all information in my mind, and only access the required information, so I can work easily.

Maybe, because we have so many solar systems in a galaxy, we do not name any solar system and co-incidentally all the ancient texts also did not name the solar system. That may be the reason my solar system does not have a name, as well as the other solar systems also do not have a name.

But my star does have a name. Every star has a name, and while I do not know the name of my star, I definitely know the names of other stars. In Sanskrit our star is known as Surya or Surya Dev. The English call him Sol but it is not a scientific name and the Greek call him Helios.

Are we alone in the Universe

All religious and ancient texts follow the same pattern in naming any solar system, they use the name of the stars to recognize any solar system. All those solar systems which have life in them are identified separately and ancient texts knew which solar system or star constellation had life similar to our planet earth.

All religions worship the Sun as a God, similarly all other solar systems, who have habitats worship their sun star as a God of all living beings.

When we refer to other solar systems in our galaxy, we refer to them from the name of their stars.

Why we know there are billions of solar systems is because at night we can see their bright light in our sky. The billions of lights specify we have so many stars each with its own solar system.

The solar systems are very much like independent countries, separated by deep space, and inaccessible due to very vast distances, making travelling between them difficult. The galaxies are like continents and the universe is like earth hosting all the countries, in continents.

Like the continents are separated by water, the solar systems, galaxies and the universe are separated by space.

Are we alone in the Universe

The Galaxies

The galaxies host the solar systems like our own nine planets solar system. We will see the arrangements of the solar system, galaxies and the universe in the dimensions chapter ahead.

Each galaxy is said to have billions of solar systems in it. We still do not know how many solar systems have habitats in them, like our own. Now we wonder, why we have so many solar systems in the first place and why we have so many stars.

23 Are we alone in the Universe

It is a very difficult question and frankly, I have no right answers for this one, and it just hits me point blank. While I see all the galaxies, that are mentioned in the ancient texts, as well as information received from the space mission, as well as exploration by the Hubble telescope, the information is common and same. The question arises, what is new that has been explored by spacecrafts and it comes to nothing.

That means God has cleverly hidden everything from us and even after going to the moon we got nothing to know about either our planet, our solar system or the galaxies. There is a big dead end everywhere and all space explorations lead to nowhere for mankind.

The galaxies contain many solar systems like ours in them and every solar system has a star at its center.

Some solar systems are new and are being built, so their stars are not fully developed. They may also die out before they are activated fully. These stars then burn out slowly. As we know nuclear reactions take place inside the stars. But sometimes these are not enough for the star to survive as ignition is not proper for them to continue burning or the star is very large, losing a lot of heat rapidly. This makes the star die out before it is fully ready to host a solar system like ours.

Stars are built continuously, in the galaxies, and there is unlimited amount of empty space in the galaxy and the universe to accommodate these stars. Once stars are ready and continue to burn, planets are added to them, and the size of the planets depends on the size of the star, its gravitational pull to hold the planets in its gravity, till a certain distance, which is called balancing.

Without this balancing in the solar systems, the planets do not stick inside the star system, and may break apart, convert into asteroids and move freely in space. To balance the position of the planets, as well as maintain its heat and temperatures, moons are added to the planets.

The placements of the moons and their quantity depends on the gravitational pull of the sun, rotational speed around the sun and many other factors including the rotation of the planets. All these calculations, I cannot provide at present but are inherent at the back of my mind.

Some of this information you will not find on Earth with scientists, as they are still exploring the Universe and they need some time to catch up.

Now, I made the planets, put them into solar systems, tested them for type 7 planets which can host life for me, and then I put all of the planets in galaxies. These galaxies I have then put into a universe which is explained in the next chapter.

This is how my advanced civilization will be of tomorrow, to will know everything it needs to know about us and our origins and about deep space. I may also discuss black holes, darkness, and time travel, travel from one dimension to another if time permits. I will also try to discuss if space is really empty or it contains dark matter, also known as ether or an ether.

The Universe

Source: Wikipedia

A Universe contains many billion galaxies in it and each of those galaxies have many solar systems. So ideally a universe contains many stars we see in the sky in the night. Because the solar systems are very large and have gravitational pulls, each solar system has to be separated from the other by a very huge distance running into trillions of

27 Are we alone in the Universe

miles till their gravitational attractions are not able to attract each other.

We call all of these objects in space as heavenly bodies including our planet Earth, these heavenly bodies are kept apart sufficiently enough so they remain in space.

The Universe needs darkness as during expansion, it utilizes heat and light. Without darkness, all of the Universe would be a hot lava forever hot and boiling. That is why we use darkness in the Universe.

The darkness absorbs light and heat. We also invented cold, as cold absorbs all the heat to make it neutral. That way darkness absorbs light and cold absorbs heat so everything remains balanced.

Nights are cold, so as to absorb all heat generated during the day, when we and the planets are exposed to the sun. Then starts the cycles of day and night. Various experiments were carried out to keep six months as day and six months as nights but they were not very successful as nights became very cold and inhospitable ins some planets like ours.

Are we alone in the Universe

In the spiritual world we make light, we combine matter and we do lot of things which are out of this world and out of science. When spirituality and science was combined, humans who learned them often misused them, so now spirituality has vanished forever, and at the most we can create robots.

Also, we now need to limit the creation of galaxies and solar systems due to limitations of space, which were in fact all created by spirituality. That is why all our texts mention the creation of all universe, galaxies, planetary systems through spiritual power. Science will forever contradict this as we have stopped the interaction if spiritual power with science.

Science contains everything textbooks, mathematics, astronomy, needed to build ships, aircrafts, mobiles, laptops, robots, but it will never be able to learn spirituality as it has been totally banned in use, after seeing multiple destructive wars in ancient times using spiritual power.

First, second, third and fourth, fifth, sixth, seventh and eighth Dimensions

All universes cannot exist together on one plane of motion, so we need dimensions to keep them apart. After making all the solar systems, galaxies and a universe to hold them, we also need parallel universes for:

1. Disposing of waste matter from one universe to another.

2. We also need a universe to create matter,

3. Another universe to hold the created matter.

The fourth universe is the one we live in.

Altogether, we need four universes.

All universes and objects are kept apart by the use of dimensions.

Some dimensions can be accessed only by deep swing or vortexes, through which spacecrafts can fly which are already present in deep space, at different locations. The first three dimensions are present on earth through which we are able to see ourselves and others and also see different kinds of objects.

Seeing everything around us is done by using dimensions and our eyes are programmed to use dimensions to understand what object it is. Our eyes do not know the names of all objects, especially those created by humans unless they are told by someone else.

The single dimension is a straight line. We have up to three dimensions in each planet as told above, and when we see outside each planet, it is the fourth dimension. Sp when we are in a space station outside our planet earth, the view we get is a four-dimensional view.

If we did not have dimensions everything would look flat to us like paper or an art drawing. Without dimensions objects cannot become live. Dimensions make objects come to live and include both living and non-living objects.

When science advances, it will include these subjects in study. Today we know only dimensions and when we will study them, we will know how it is used.

This straight line below is a single dimension, which allows us to see everything on earth.

Example of a single dimension:

_____

Two dimensions means a triangle, rectangle or square box and many other similar objects.

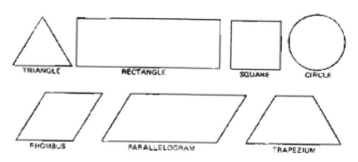

All above objects are example of a two dimension.

Three dimension means the following:

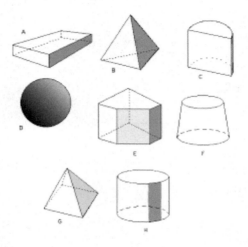

The following is the summary from single dimension to three dimensions.

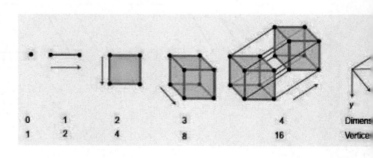

33 Are we alone in the Universe

We do not travel in the first three dimensions as they are omnipresent and known to us.

Our view of the land from an airplane is three dimension and not fourth dimension and can be seen by birds and other flying objects.

Source: Wikipedia

Source: Wikipedia

Then comes the fourth dimension, that is what we see from the roof of our room or an outside view of the Earth. We can see fourth dimension, when we are in spacecraft flying above the Earth or from a space station.

Source: Wikipedia

The outside views of a solar system is fifth dimension.

Source: Wikipedia

This is an example of a sixth dimension below when we move out of the galaxies.

An outer view of any galaxy has to be called seven dimensions. The word seven seas and seven births and also used in many different religious and ancient texts is more or less similar to this dimension and its meaning of afterlife and souls meeting again and again in different seven-dimension galaxies. Remember there are billions and billions of galaxies, but only four universes.

All my written text and information will be pretty accurate, and I avoid writing wrong information and always cross check my works with other information from reliable sources about everything written here whether about time, space, planets, stars and everything has been cross checked before I wrote this book for you.

The seventh dimension is a cluster of galaxies.

The simple way to understand dimensions is that they go on increasing, as you go higher and higher. When you are sleeping, it is first dimension, when you wake up and stand, it is second dimension and when a bird sees you, he sees you in third dimension. That is why we need special glasses to convert two dimensional objects to three dimensions.

When we are above the Earth, it will be four dimensions, and as we move out of the solar system, we move into fifth dimension and when we move out of our Galaxy, it is sixth dimension. The seventh dimension is the last one, when we are outside of all the universes that exist.

Example of a eighth dimension

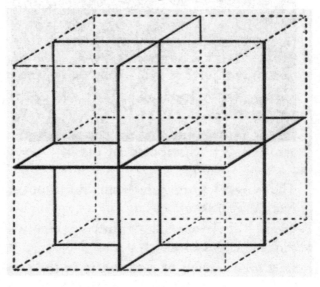

There are four universes on each axis is being illustrated by an image as below:

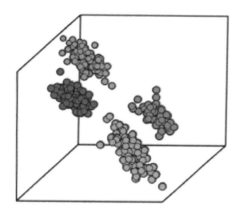

My eighth dimension has four parallel universes as shown above and each parallel universe is distinct and different from the other.

The green color can be considered as our live universe, the starting point is the matter, in light brown color above, then, it collects into more solid matter in blue color, then converts into the rock-colored matter.

After that the rock matter gets converted to planets and stars, which host living beings and elements and compounds in green. When the star is created, it is ignited with the fire from other stars and the fire is taken from an existing star and taken to a huge planet which has all flammable material in it, like the one we see on Jupiter. So to make a sun, we need a very big planet more or less the size of Jupiter or even bigger, have all burning gases, fuels and then continue a chain nuclear reaction much like our forest fires, which then burns for thousands of years or more.

The voyager space craft went out of the solar system, but has not yet gone out of the universe or even the galaxy. It was launched by NASA, first to study the planets and then to study the outer solar system of ours.

The eighth dimension has a Universe on each axial plane. I believe in only four parallel universes exist. Beyond this eighth universe there is nothing but empty space and no matter exists beyond the eight dimensions. I do not need anything beyond my eight dimensions and we will never need anything above the eight dimensions ever for millions and billions of years from now.

Everything is circular in the universe, which means we come back to the same place from where we started. For example, our home, we go to work, to market, parks, hospitals, government offices and we come back to home. Our universe works in the same way, the soul travels from one universe to another and comes back to the same place, again to go on another journey. The planets, stars, solar systems, galaxies all come back to the same positions.

Like the speed of various animals and beings on earth, all heavenly bodies have different speeds. Even animals return to their homes, if they have a home. For planets or stars who do not have a home or are isolated, they are called falling stars or asteroids much the same like our wandering animals and gypsies who have no home.

Each Universe looks like this as shown below, and is not rectangular. The rectangular shapes above are shown just for understanding, how the Universes are arranged in symmetrical axis. At some places on the earth, we can see the other galaxies of our universe also.

Are we alone in the Universe

Source: Wikipedia

The universe is not rectangular in shape as shown in my images, and it is only meant to show locations and orientations using these rectangular shapes in the images I have used here in this book. The universe is more like the colors shown above, but has swirling motion around itself and its epic center.

The Lord of the Universe - God

The Lord of the universe is the one we call God; he is a supernatural being. The meaning itself means natural like us, but a super human being. He is all matter, omnipresent everywhere, and can acquire as many different shapes as he desires.

Like we have presidents and prime ministers and other leaders, we also have God. Without our God, our galaxies cannot run smoothly. The reason we had different Gods is a thing of the past and now we are more into believing the one Universal God.

Through all our Gods we worship the ultimate God much like we worship our local leaders and ministers. Our leaders and ministers in ultimate worship their own leaders. It is up to you to worship him directly or through your own religious God.

When we try to do supremacy over God, by making spacecrafts, satellites, weapons of mass destruction, robots, artificial intelligence, mass communication, our ability is limited, first by our human bodies, which has limited ability to travel outside of our solar systems.

Second, the time required to travel large distances to reach him, and harm him or his domain, with our spacecrafts and weapon systems is difficult and impossible. So, even if we learn more and more about our universe, we should never think of being more superior than him. He is all almighty and powerful beyond our wildest imaginations. He is not like the Hollywood movies either.

The gods shown in the movies do not match with our gods. Their brains are at peace and they are calm at all times. They are gentle and ever forgiving, but because human nature is not perfect and we are prone to hate and fighting, we cannot see the real him in us. Even aliens say, we know there is God, but we have never seen him.

God is compassionate and does not harm us even when we try to harm him in many ways by showing our technological superiority because we will only destroy ourselves, like we have done many times in the past.

But past history has shown, we tend to try to harm God and also the people who believe in him. You may be surprised to know, God does not like problematic people and prefers ordinary citizens to go higher to his kingdom, who can do no harm to other fellow citizens and have led an ordinary life of simplicity.

As the God of the Universe, for him, our Earth is only a small district, like the ones we have in our countries. The galaxies are the states for him. While we recognize our own presidents and prime ministers, we do not recognize the supreme God.

These things were told to me during childhood telepathically or it just came into my mind, I do not know from where all this information comes, when I was around 10 years of age. I don't have any proofs, so do not ask me for proofs, since these are more telepathic and not visual.

Any prime minister or a president of a country, does not go directly to meet someone, unless under special conditions. You will not see them going freely, and are supposed to move under supervision. When top leaders do that, God also operates in the same way.

It is up to you to believe, whether it is true or not. Earlier, the Gods nominated the kings, and the kings passed on the ownership from generation to generation downwards. But with times, it was tough to keep up with wars, change of ownership, conquests, when countries changed hands and so on. We have governments, whom we elect and we monitor whether they work properly or not and change these governments every five or six years. God has left it on us to decide, which government is better and change them if they are unfit for us with another one which may be better. Some governments still have kings or queens, as their status quo did not change and we did not feel they need to be replaced with modern day type governments. When buildings are new, the builder visits them regularly, till they are finished and completed. When our Earth was new, we were visited by extra-terrestrial beings

Are we alone in the Universe

Time, Space, Matter and Energy

The only thing that binds empty space is binding energy. Different binding energies combine empty space into matter. The more the binding energy used, the more solid is the matter, and more is the heat required to break its components.

Do we know how elements are formed, do we know how matter is formed, do we know from where does the rocks, mountains, gases come from to make the planet and stars. We know nothing. Every element or atom has empty space and every nucleus of an atom is also empty.

Like our solar systems, each element in the periodic table we know, has the same pattern inside it. While we consider an atom to be a single entity, a atom is same as our solar system, having electrons rotating around its nucleus in the centre.

Hydrogen is called an atom and oxygen is another atom. The two combines in the ratio of two hydrogen atoms plus an oxygen atom to make water. This water is supposed to be neutral and combine with everything we have on earth. It is the basis of all life existing anywhere in the universe. No atom can combine with another atom openly and has rules. If i allowed all atoms to combine freely, then it would be catastrophic and chain reactions would occur.

Different atoms have different binding energies and need different environments to combine with each other. When atoms combine, they release heat of reaction. This heat released during the reaction is the excess heat.

Atoms combing to form compounds and water is a compound. Water is the most stable compound and not all compounds are as stable as water and some compounds break down into individual atoms when heated. Water does not break down into hydrogen and oxygen, on heating and it vaporizes into steam if heated and goes into ice form if kept refrigerated.

Water does not harm our body at the right temperature, and only if it is too hot or cold does it harm our skin.

Inter dimensional travel - The cycle of life and death

In the cycle of life and death, we move from one last Universe to the first Universe. The four universes are the spiritual universe which comes first, second is the matter converting stage or second universe, third stage has only matter and no life an no galaxies and the last one is our universe which has all matter in form of solar systems, galaxies and stars in them.

The working of the universe is much like a factory, where matter is created in this first universe, moves to the second universe, then it is shifted to the fourth universe for creating the stars, planets and the solar system. The third Universe is the garbage, where our souls go after we die and for recycling.

The same principle is followed by our human bodies, plants, animals, factories, waste treatment plants, everywhere there is symmetry of operation.

51 Are we alone in the Universe

Everything in the inner world, by inner world it means the world we live in, inside the planet Earth is symmetrical. Also, in the outer world also which we cannot see, it is symmetrical. What we think of as symmetrical is different, from that which actually exists because we see things from inside and not from outside. Most of the time we are conscious of ourselves and what other people think of us and what we think of others.

To come out of this illusion of thinking about everything, we need to see ourselves from outside instead of inside, that is what every religious text says all the time, but we never listen and remain forever in the illusions of space and time. That is why we miss seeing the dimensions, even when they are so near to us.

What has Science discovered?

What information is there in the science was already present in the religious texts given to us by God. The old age civilizations already developed the mathematics, chemistry, nearby stars, galaxies and most of the things we know today about things in the Universe.

What science did was utilizing this information to create objects like mobiles, laptops spacecraft, vehicles, buildings, houses, airplanes, cars, trucks, packing and drying natural food.

Scientists are still not able to make any type of artificial food. The medicines are also extracted from plants and artificial medicines are harmful and taking too much of them can cause numerous side-affects like vomiting and nausea. Those artificial medicines are also a copy of medicines present in the plants. What did we actually invent is a big question.

We do only exploration of things already present on this planet or on other planets.

The Sun as a God and the Creator

Source: Wikipedia

The sun is also a God in the true sense, as without him, our life on this planet would not exist. If it was false, then there would be life on Mars and on other planets more distant from the sun. Too much hot everything turns into vapors and too much cold things turn into ice.

All cellular organisms, need the energy of the sun. Sun is life for all cells. The human body is made up of billions of cells which take energy from the sun. Plants take energy from the sun, so do animals.

I do not remember everything in exact as they exist, but I am conscious of those things I know, and can write on most of the topics, which I have read and they have become inbuilt in my memory.

I have read all about those scientists that have made all of the discoveries we have today. For me God is still the biggest scientist and I shall produce God as the scientist in the later part of this book and I will show what he created and how he created all living organisms[1].

But I cannot remember everything that I read accurately with dates, but I known those things at the back of my mind.

I still cannot create things even after knowing so much. It just beats me. I could only make some small software's, make

websites in a few languages, write articles and books and maybe make a few electronic

_____
[1]

gadgets at home. But creation beats me by a very huge margin.

We always oppose touching human or plant embryos, and while we are allowed to study them for medicine, anything to do with research and reproduction is illegal. Mankind was kind enough to ban its testing and reproduction and cloning which was a sensible step.

Had the testing of human embryos not been banned, it would have had catastrophic implications. Already mankind is filled with a burden of a huge population to feed, and not all of the humans have houses and easy access to food.

While we have reproduction, as death is an eminent thing, so we pass on our dreams and aspirations to our siblings. Through reproduction we continue to live in another way that will be hard to explain. But reproduction is another way of living again and again as reproduction is a part that comes from our own bodies.

Type 7 Planets which have Life in them.

Life can exist only on Type 7 planets. These planets have the optimum temperature, neutral atmosphere, enough moisture in the environment and all of the necessary elements in the atmosphere required to sustain life.

For this to happen they should be equidistant from the sun, meaning neither too far nor near enough. If they are too far, they become very cold and have only ice, and if they are too near, everything is hot or gets burned.

So that is why there is life only on Earth and not on other planets as these are not hospitable foe life to exist. Neither can bacteria or other multi-cellular organisms exist on these planets and die to the harsh environments.

Actually, to create a type 7 solar system, which I will also discuss in detail later, I need to experiment with making many different solar systems similar to like our own. When we make these solar systems with all the planets in them, it still is not suitable to host life unless it matches the requirement of my Type 7 solar system.

That may be one probability, why I do not see any nearby solar systems similar to my own.

So many of my solar systems go waste, even after I make them nicely, making the sun, then making the planets, putting the planets in orbits around the sun or the star. The reason which I explained above is some of my planets are either too hot or too cold. If their temperatures match to my neutral requirements, when I add the other things such as inclination, orbit speed, moons, the balance is not the same.

All done, then when I check those planets, there are a lot of things missing in them. For example, some are too hot as the planet is close to the sun. Some planets are very cold if they are far away from the sun, so they do not match my requirements to host life. So that may be one of the reasons why I have millions of solar systems and galaxies, because to get one perfect solar system, I need to experiment with different galaxies.

The atmosphere of the Earth is also harsh like many other planets on this solar system as well as planets on other solar systems.

But it has an additional protection called the ozone layer.

The ozone layer also known as oxygen 3 protects the Earth from the harmful radiations of the sunlight from entering the earth's atmosphere. This ozone layer was protective enough, because we did not have chemical factories when our planet was made into an environment friendly living system.

Without this ozone layer to protect us, the type 7 category of our planet is not enough for us to survive and as soon as the ozone layer depletes, so do we cease to exist. We are no different from other planets, when we say we have a good atmosphere. No ozone means no life on earth.

Ozone is good only for protection from radiation and if inhaled, ozone harms the lungs causing shortness of breath, coughing or lungs damage. It is present in only the topmost layer of the earth.

Plants also make ozone and I believe the ozone is made in the night in addition to oxygen, which they make in the daytime. The ozone is made in small quantities by the plants which go up to the topmost layers and compensate for any loss in the ozone layer depletion.

I will explain all of this in the nature cycle part by part making it easier for you to understand.

We now stress very much on the protection of our environment as due to the imbalance created by the chemical factories and burning of fossil fuels, the ozone layer is getting damaged more than it should.

One way is to either plant more trees, or use less fossil fuels such as petrol, diesel, coal and burn less trees. Plantation of trees on a large scale is costly. God found an alternative way to make humans grow trees, seeing the future destruction, he invented growing plants for food. In this way every year we grow food from plants and then again plant them for the coming season next year, compensating the environment in some way.

But chemical factories and fossil fuels still generate more carbon dioxide, and if ignored, the carbon dioxide built up will enlarge the hole in the ozone layer. allowing the sun's radiation to enter freely and melt ice in the polar regions.

If due to global warming, the ice in the polar regions melt, this will cause the rise of water in the seas and oceans, and then this water will enter the rivers. That is why many countries are part of this global warming initiative, to reduce the production of these gases which were harmful to the environment.

The gases used in refrigeration were found harmful to the earth's atmosphere as they could travel higher up of released and harm the protective ozone layer above earth. Other refrigeration gases were discovered, but some developing countries continued to use the old type of gases in their refrigeration equipments.

Industries who took the green initiatives, by planting more trees, reducing use of harmful gases and reduced carbon dioxide emissions in developing countries were given a monetary compensation to encourage them to stop harming the environment by the rich countries.

Also, since the rich countries also had huge factories releasing smoke and carbon dioxide, they paid monetary compensation to poor countries, to go green and balance the pollution.

If that happens, the same thing will happen like it is said in the time of Moses. Moses was a prophet of God in whose time the great flood was predicted, when most of the ice in the polar regions melted. leading to entire planet getting flooded with water for many hundreds of years.

Moses was told of the event and asked to take as many animals and humans as possible and built a very big ship and shift to higher lands.

Only those survived at the time of Moses, who shifted to mountains and higher rocks and hills. They came down when water levels came down and there was a period of darkness for many years.

The atmosphere of Earth has approximately 78 % nitrogen, 21 % oxygen, 0.9 % Argon and rest consists of ozone, carbon monoxide and carbon dioxide, hydrogen and other gases. We had to keep nitrogen in the atmosphere of the Earth as 78 % because oxygen is highly inflammable gas and without nitrogen present, there would be flames and fire everywhere on Earth. While making the atmosphere of the Earth, we kept this in mind. We also added 0.9 % argon, which is also an inert gas to balance the nitrogen. This combination was found suitable after a lot of experiments by God, the creator and not by a big bang theory, which we will discuss later in this book.

No big bang theory created the Universe in the first instant, and if it did, the big bang was created by God, much in the same way we blow up hills with explosives to get rocks, for using them in making buildings.

Before making the Universe, God had to blow up an entire mountain of matter, much bigger than hundreds of planets. These rocks were then molded into round shapes and slung into rotation around the sun.

Matter does not combine on its own to make mountains, or planets as is evident and if it does, there is no proof. I will also discuss this as a separate chapter.

Environment on Mars

Mars does not have an ozone layer, which I need to make humans life live, and move around freely on the planet, or does it have ozone or did it have ozone.

Mars has almost 95 % carbon dioxide and around 2 % of Nitrogen and 1.9 % Argon and other gases. Mars is a raw planet like Earth was thousands of centuries back before it became what it is today.

The extreme temperatures on Mars go below -60 degrees Celsius at the poles and in other areas, the temperature in summer is only 20 degrees at the maximum. This is not enough for plants to survive and impossible for human beings as there is no oxygen present there.

It is said there is radiation on Mars, which prevents it from having a life-giving system like ours. For this first let's study radioactivity.

I had decided to make Mars a habitat ever since I was a child and the thoughts came to me as early as the 1980's. The thoughts were not my own and seem to come from somewhere unknown, which I have never been able to discover and my knowledge collected over the years to what I am writing now in this book.

Though I know, I will not be able to do it in this birth or ever, it is just an imaginative feeling i have, that is why I wrote this book in case Mars becomes a habitat, I had imagined every since I was a young child.

The ozone layer on Mars is very weak and so is water vapor which can also block ultraviolet rays of the sun. Due to this the radiation from the sun reaches the soil on Mars and destroys any organic molecules present there. So, how do I make life on Mars, the same as on Earth.

Mars does not have plants, and neither it has been established if it has single cell or multi-cellular organisms in its soil or can survive in those harsh temperatures.

Mars also needs magnetism at its poles in addition to ozone to protect life from radiation effects, and there appears to be no magnetism there or it is very less or undetectable. High levels of radiation cause cancer. Humans can absorb 200 rads of radiation per year and presently, we absorb around 1 rads per year.

If I take elements from Earth, and shift them on Mars, obviously the Earth will not survive as there is a balance of elements on Earth. The entire atmosphere of Mars cannot be made using elements from Earth. Neither, can I shift compounds from Earth to Mars in large quantities. It would be utter foolishness.

If Earth loses elements and compounds in large quantities, it would imbalance the nature and the natural environment making most of the areas of Earth become deserts.

I would need very large ships for moving my materials from Earth to Mars. Building small colonies for the first hundreds of years, like the greenhouses, is feasible to me, which would require continuous replacement of goods every month to maintain those colonies much like how we maintain our space station rotating around the planet Earth.

These colonies would have everything we need for life to survive on Mars. A space station like building on Mars fully filled with oxygen and a artificial atmosphere, cabins, generators, electricity points, rovers.

My initial colony would have to consists of at least two hundred people and the building would need to be protected from the harmful radiations of the sun.

The Elements of Life and how it got created on Earth

Are we alone in the Universe

We have a total of 118 discovered elements. By elements, I mean, hydrogen, helium oxygen, nitrogen, carbon, argon, neon and so on. In addition to being an author, I also have a four-year degree in chemical engineering, so I have additional studies or specialization in one major subject.

Most of these elements exist in gaseous and liquid forms and have low boiling points of less than a hundred degrees Celsius.

So, since most of these elements are used by the cellular organisms to build plants, animals and human beings, they are there in liquid and gaseous forms. Had we been very near the sun, the liquid elements would be in vapor forms, making them inaccessible to the cellular organisms.

Like the three primary colors of Red, Yellow and Blue there are these 118 primary elements. The three colors red, yellow and blue after combining with each other produce all the other secondary colors. The reason we see different colors is due to the fact that when light passes through those materials, it gets displaced, also called as refraction. The amount by which light bends makes us see different colors, even though they are of the same color.

Similarly, the 118 elements combine in various ways to make different compounds. Oxygen and Hydrogen are elements or atoms, but combine to make water. We can see water but we cannot see hydrogen and oxygen.

If everything was invisible, we would have not been able to see anything on Earth. Basically, everything is invisible, we only see them when they combine to form compounds like water, salts, rocks, minerals and so on.

All plants, animals and birds as well as the environment was made neutral and all that existed had a neutral ph of 7, because we did not want to disturb the environment in any way for thousands of years.

We have colors for all compounds and gaseous elements are not visible to us.

Are we alone in the Universe

Elements are like single cellular organisms, and only the gaseous are invisible to our eyes. Some examples of gaseous elements are nitrogen, oxygen, hydrogen and helium all of which are in gas form. These elements when converted into liquid forms using high pressures can be seen, but only in liquid forms.

Compounds such as water, acids, salts, various types of chemicals can be seen by us as these are not in form of gases. If and when these become gases, we can hardly see them except as a vapor like steam.

Metals are always solid and can always be seen. They are hardly ever there in isolated forms and are mostly found combined together. We can smell some gases and those gases which do not have smell cannot be detected by humans or animals. Mostly if a gas is poisonous, it has smell, to give us a warning to run away.

If a gas is harmless for our bodies, it will not have smell. All gases which have smell or taste are harmful in large quantities and less damaging if present in smaller concentrations. No scientist discovered these things and this were invented by God only and not me or you.

The Earth and its seasons

Are we alone in the Universe

The planets we see in the sky were static, as assumed in prehistoric times as well in some of the ancient histories, means they were always there in one place. This is very much like apparent rotation of movement, which you can easily see, when you are there in a railway station platform.

When you stand static on a railway platform, and as the train moves out of the platform, it appears that the train is static and you are moving while the train is not moving at all.

Another view you get to see is when you are sitting in the train and observing the platform, when the train is leaving the platform slowly. There you see the platform moving and it appears you are static.

Another, true example of the Earth's rotation is when you move around yourself in a circle, many times over and then stop suddenly. Then you will find that the Earth is actually rotating and is not static as believed in earlier times.

The ancient people believed that the Sun was also static and did not have rotation. There was no explanation of the day and night. But they believed that only the moon was moving, and causing day and night.

I myself and the ancient people believed that only the moons of the planets moved, and that caused day and night and the seasons. The moon blocked the rays of the sun at different places, at different times, leading to the variations in temperatures.

While the high tides and certain periods of day and night got accounted for, I could not account for the equators and the north pole and the south poles and the extreme hotness at the equators and extreme coldness at the poles. Even though I fitted these into the rotation of the moon, it only said that since the moon could not cover the corners, so the poles should have been hot and the equators should have been cold. But actually, it is the opposite.

I have not explored how much sunlight the poles receive, and if indeed the rotation of the moon does obstruct the sun's rays to the poles, then maybe Earth may be a static place and not round.

Another, theory that I have is that is flat at the poles, so it helps to keep ice there all around, and its flat surface minimizes it getting exposed to the sun's radiations.

The reason that the poles get less exposure to the sun is not because they are obstructed by the moon as in case of all other areas of our planet, but because the Earth is tilted at an axis of 23.5 degrees and is not exactly vertical.

Most of these theories are my own and may or not match with actual scientific evidences. I take all blames on myself for predicting such theories whether true or false. So due to the tilt and assuming a flat surface at the poles it helps to keep the temperatures low.

When it is summer at north pole it is winter at the south pole and vice versa. The temperatures even in summer in the north or south poles is below 13 degrees, which they call summer and in winters they may be anything below 4 degrees. So that is how ice manages to survive on the poles.

There is also very high magnetism at the poles, where north pole has positive magnetism and the north pole has negative magnetism. This helps to find out the directions for ships to travel and for a compass to work.

Earth is having the most carbon dioxide, which is very much needed for plant life to survive and when plants survive so do humans and planets. Without carbon dioxide, there cannot be plant life.

Plants absorb very little carbon dioxide, and release oxygen. The humans and other animals take in the oxygen so that is the balance nature has made for both to survive. If plants and animals both needed oxygen to survive, it would be disastrous.

For all planets to survive and exist, they should have liquid rock in the core, which is hot and full of fire. That is the center of every planet. The hot lava leaks from some places in the planets. These areas where the hot lava leaks are called volcanoes.

All of us humans and animals on planet earth, are also rotating around the sun at a speed of approximately 67,000 miles per hour. We never felt tired while moving around year after years and season after season. While we do get tired from working in our offices and working at home, we hardly get tired at moving around the Sun.

We have made innumerable discoveries and inventions but have been unable to either create ourselves or do anything that is beyond imagination.

The Nature of life and living organisms

Life lives and thrives in only the organic form, it means all living beings have most of the elements in common, which include carbon, oxygen, nitrogen and small amounts of hydrogen, helium and argon. So, what is there in the plants is also present in the atmosphere which we call as air.

All cellular organisms including bacteria work in the same way and also have the same biological structure with a inner nucleus, and a DNA making factory. Humans and animals, including plants are multi cellular organisms having many billions of cells.

The factories inside our bodies are constantly producing DNA and other substances and release the waste materials from the kidneys as well as from the anuses. There are different methods uses for plants to remove waste products. The waste of bees is honey and is sweet and can be consumed, a feature not there in other organisms.

The day we stop feeding our bodies or mini factories, we will lose life due to hunger and our factory will close down. Our bodies carry their own treatment plants and continuously need the waste products to be removed almost every day. This is how we survive.

While, I know everything about life, single and multi-cellular cells, I will limit this information for later on slowly, one bite at a time.

We have different cells at different locations in our bodies, similar to a reception in an office, then the main plant, a waste treatment plant like in a factory and the management.

In our bodies, the mind is the management, the mouth is the reception, which receives all incoming material into the body and the stomach is the main plant which handles production and sends it for packing or to the waste treatment plant the kidneys and the anus.

Different animals have different taste receptors, so the receptionist is different for each class of animal. The taste receptors inside the living beings decide which type of foods to eat. For vegetarian receptors like goats, deer's, elephants can only eat and thrive on plants.

The other living factories like lions, wolves, jackals, eagles, tigers and others thrive on other animals. Humans have a choice to either thrive on plants or animals or both. So this is pre-defined.

Scientists experimented with feeding cattle with flesh of other animals and the result was mad cow disease. When you do not listen to the thing's nature has designed, this is what happens. Humans eating vegetarian or non-vegetarian is also pre-decided.

The Journey of Life on Earth

Are we alone in the Universe

The first known civilization on Earth is said to have existed 10,000 years back according to some historians.

The current population of Earth is said to be close to 7.5 billion human beings and around 20 to 30 billion of animals and more than 500 billion plants.

This is the kind of life we have on Earth. Since we need plants to survive, the plants should at least be more than 1000 times our population, and if this reduces our chances of being alive becomes less.

In this way as plants decrease, so there is no protection from the radiation of the Sun on all living beings. This is true because it is very difficult for humans to survive in deserts where there are hardly any trees present. Only cactus and a few other plants like the date palm trees are found to exist in such hot climates.

For humans to survive, we need trees everywhere even in places like the north and the south pole, humans are not able to survive. due to the absence of trees.

The absence of plants causes severe temperatures of hot and cold. Even animals need plants to survive and animals cannot survive on other animals alone.

Harappa and Mohenjo-Daro and other ancient civilizations like the Atlantis.

The advanced civilizations of the ancient past like Harappa and Mohenjo-Daro simply got destroyed, as these civilizations were harnessing the natural power of our planet. They built dams from earth, and knew how to make bricks and brick houses using lime as cement.

The civilizations built advanced societies and government like we have today. But, when there were excessive rains in that area due to seasonal shifts of the moon, other planet gravities affecting our gravitational systems, their canals got flooded with water and the entire city getting submerged in water.

There were protective walls to the ancient cities of Harappa and Mohenjo-Daro cities, so when water flooded the entire city, there was no escape routes like boats, with the entire civilization vanishing.

After a few years the entire water dried up in these ancient cities, due to another seasonal change, and then we got to know about existence of those cities. After that the cities were still under the same mud, they used to build these cities and then after the archeologist removed these mud excavations, we got to see the ruins as of now.

The Atlantis is an example of another ancient civilization which maybe existed on a planet in the island in Atlantic Ocean. The civilization was advanced, but was built in such a way, that in times of a disaster like ocean floods, and high tides, due to the same seasonal changes, the entire city would got flooded under water.

The Atlantis is believed to be an island that existed approximately 10,000 years back and got destroyed by a tsunami in the ocean. It was first mentioned by Plato, a Greek historian at around 400 B.C. which is 2400 years from today. The Harappa or Indus valley civilization was said to have existed around 1500 B.C.

I am never interested in which civilizations exist, I am more interested in how did Plato know about the existence of Atlantis. John. Fleet discovered the existence of Harappa civilization in 1912, so there was some proof, which then led to excavations of the ancient cities.

Plato, the Greek historian appears to have borrowed the story from Egyptian historical books. Then appeared mystical stories of the island believed to be in the Atlantic Ocean.

I have to cross check everything I write, so it is authentic and not based on rumors and superstition. That is how I have explored the entire earth, searching and learning of everything sitting at my place. I eat knowledge in the same place like people eat different kinds of food and then as I wanted the internet happened giving me access to all the information, I needed to write everything in a series of books at one single place.

So, I believe, the internet was invented for me, and when I write and compile information, I have everything on my fingertips to cross check all philosophers' and historians that may have existed on the planet earth. I even had to study philosophy for this.

I will not be able to write about some of those ancient civilizations in entirely, only because, I have lack of time and maybe in my later series, I may go back and research them feeding you with more interesting information for your brains just like myself.

I have not put myself in remembering exact dates and times and when in personal interviews, I hope I am not asked to do so. I can, if I want remember exact sequences and historical dates, but I prefer to skip them for now. Maybe, later on, I will convert my mind to remember all dates and events as they happen today or happened hundreds of thousands of years back.

I mentioned the Indus valley civilizations, is located in Pakistan and Northwest India, because proofs exist of them even today. Ruins of Atlantis are not found enough for it to exist as real.

The story of Atlantis was passed down from generations to generations till it got through the Greek historian or philosopher Plato who penned it down into paper around 2400 years back.

Thereafter, it became an object of interest the world over and the fever has not died yet. Then, after reading all over, I found nothing, I went over to the Bermuda triangle believing the Atlantis city was under the

Bermuda triangle where I found some scientists the world over agrees on that theory.

The Bermuda triangle and Atlantis and the Aryans

I have made my own theories, reading information from different theories. But they do not match together, as I want. The information was like the rubric cube of different colors, and when I tried to match them, they did not.

But I tried my best and that does not mean I failed. But my theories will be not be recognized or accepted as I am not a known person, or a scientist, or a historian or a philosopher. I may be only recognized as a small-time writer or an unknown author.

After studying the Aryans, I had to study Hitler, who was very much interested in my Aryans. Many of these things, i have studied in childhood, where information was hardly available and I am talking of the years from 1980 to 1990 buying second hand books, when I studied all types if Earth history, then expanded it to studying on the internet after it became freely available.

I spent a lot on studying, and knowledge comes at a price and it is not free and there are internet charges and costs of buying new gadgets every time in addition to purchasing books.

I used public libraries and the library of my school and college to read things, I did not know or were missing. So, Hitler, why he mentioned of Aryans. The Aryans made religious books which were not there in German history.

I read a few stories of the mythology of the Germans and their characters did not match the Aryan characters. Then I read Greek mythology, their epics are similar to the Ramayana and Mahabharata that they are long as that of the Aryans, and found no similarity in the stories. The famous Greek epics, I read was the Odyssey and a Sumerian epic the Gilgamesh.

All of the epics depict heroic wars, some between nations and some in search of love, travelling through high seas and rough lands in the Greek epics.

The Indian epics depict great wars, internal feuds with the family, or between sister nations for supremacy.

This was all unassembled rubric cube for me, nothing fitting to the other in these mythologies of whether the Greeks, or the

Aryans, and the colors on the sides of the cube are not same with those civilizations.

Greek civilization, I have exemplified as being white in color, Aryan in black color, Egyptian in blue color and so on. The colors matched for each civilization, but they did not match with the other civilizations and Greek does not match Aryan and neither Egyptian matches the Greek civilization or the Sumerian.

The Aryans, Greeks, Egyptians and others had records of their being in existence through monuments, temples and other historical buildings which also exist today. You can read more about them in my other book on Bermuda Triangle and Altantis.

Our consciousness and the gravitational pull on the planets in the solar system.

90   Are we alone in the Universe

This will be a small chapter here, and I will devote time to this later on in this book, or later in another series. This is something about how the planets work and how our minds work due to the planets and their positions in the solar system.

Our minds are part of the great consciousness which we call God. We had to establish governments as our earlier experiences with humans managing on their own was difficult. Then we had tribes, a group of humans who learned to live together and established small traditions like building houses and getting married instead of living in caves.

God is the entire consciousness, in which we live. Everyone, from animals, humans and plants live under that part of the central consciousness. After, becoming small groups, humans became slightly powerful, hoarding lands that were free to roam around. Now presently, with the advent of governments all free land is said to belong to the governments of respective countries except Africa.

If we meddle with Africa, we will lose our ancient traditions and all proof of our existence on Earth will vanish into thin air just like Atlantis or the Indus valley civilizations which were destroyed by Tsunami and not human wars.

We need Africa to be like it is, as the environment of Africa protects the environment of the Earth and the pollution in big cities and huge chemical factories everywhere on this planet.

We perform, with respect to each other, as well as our environment and the status of our family. Every family, rich or poor performs according to its position in the society and each society performs according to the government and country it lives in and the food habits it has.

This consciousness applies to the religious festivals and traditions also. The festivals, and religious ceremonies are bases of each culture and differ from place to place and from country to country. The only reason, the religions and traditions become same is when the people have travelled themselves and settled in other places than their own.

This includes conquests, invasions or the countries themselves absorbing the religion as it did not have its own established traditions.

This is proof consciousness travels everywhere only through our minds. So then why are all minds not morally good and why do some people do crimes or do bad activities.

Bad activities exist because of circumstances. Due to sudden outbursts of anger, or an attack humans kill each other, some fight in wars or defend themselves in an attack. This sudden attack of bad events, develops a bad nature. This carries on with other people coming into contact with them and spreading the bad activities just like viruses do.

The viruses are harmful substances and organisms just like we have in our body. These cellular organisms became the habitat of poisonous weeds and plants feeding on them and came into contact with humans by travelling from those places to human habitats.

Many of those viruses are still in deep jungles and when humans travel there and come back, they carry those viruses into modern cities and societies. Some viruses are originated form animals and come into human contact from animals also.

The 5000-year cycle of Time

It is believed that there is a 5000 years cycle of life on Earth also called the time cycle. What was interesting was that I found this cycle common in many religions including the Mayan civilization. Different civilizations have the same concept of space and time but all lead and believe in the 5000 years cycle.

The 5000 years cycle is like sewage water, when our environment gets highly polluted with many types of contaminations where it becomes impossible to sustain life.

It is like you are pure water at the beginning of the cycle and at the end of the 5000 years you are technologically advanced, using up all the fossil fuels in large quantities, polluting the entire air, and have so many factories, spitting smoke and polluting the waters heavily with poisonous chemicals, and the Earth is flooded with many humans and animals which are difficult to sustain.

The governments flood the people with so many taxes, which are impossible to pay and government expenses become very high so no one can afford them. The cost of space exploration becomes unaffordable and money becomes a scarce commodity.

Earlier God was able to interfere and restore things back to normal, but ever since technology becomes powerful, it is able to challenge our very origins, interfering with our embryos, cloning and even searching for planets where we can live in case the Earth planet dies due to excessive use of its planetary resources.

Every time God has come on this planet, he was always challenged and attacked. The governments at that time attacked God and tried to prove he did not exist and it was with great difficulty that people recognized his power and he was asked to show miracles to prove himself.

Today, if God appears again, he would have to prove himself more powerful than our technologically advanced than us. Our governments would oppose him in tooth and nail as people would stop paying taxes or pay for the government expenditure. That is the reason that governments fear God.

The end of this 5000 years cycle is around the 23rd century, hardly 200 years from now. I do not know if I will be alive to see that event. That is the time when all the fossil fuels like petrol, diesel, coal would end on Earth. When these things end, we would have to go back to using bullock carts and horses and maybe bicycles may still continue to exist.

The Environment on Earth

That is why now governments focus on the regenerative sources of energy, and preserving our environment so we can live longer. Earlier, government wanted taxes or money, but now since all stock of fuels has been sold, they want to preserve whatever is left, before shifting to other forms of energy sources. Now, they offer taxation waiver for solar energy and other renewably sources of energy, but when solar energy becomes developed like our fossil fuels, they will also be charged heavily.

The solar energy will soon suck out a major portion of the energy of the sun, making our planet hotter and hotter. We also use wind power which diverts the natural winds, which is now changing our seasons like rain, winters and summers.

The seasons very much depend on the directions the winds flow. When we use large fans to drain wind power, these fans change the air direction and currents in the same way as the fans in our room do. This makes the timings of the seasons late. For example, at one city there was rains every

March, it shifted to every June in a few years and then to around July every year in a span of thirty years.

That is how winds affect the seasons, no winds mean no seasons.

Our origin on Earth

I studied a lot about our origins myself, which will take me more than a hundred books to explain. But I like to explain things in short and make it easy for everyone to read and understand.

Throughout my books, I will try to explain as many things as possible, about our origins, origins of the plants, animals, nature and origin of all elements on earth.

All these things were a banned subject, until now, and with advancement in technology, people do not feel inhibited about knowing or learning these things.

I am sure after telling you everything about ourselves, our origins and our ancestors, mankind continues to be a good society with good moral values and will become more stronger morally.

The goal of God is not that humans be highly developed in technology, as technology will bring about only destruction everywhere which includes atomic and nuclear technology. These are not needed in moral society.

Everything was given to us, plants for food, fishes, rains for water, rivers, oceans for travelling to other lands and many other things. Human beings were created with different features, none of them looking the same so we were not like robots. Had we been the same like robots, we would not have been able to recognize each other and that would be convincing.

Nuclear technology is become like poison, and the more poison a nation has the less it is venerable to attack by the other nation. It is being used as a tool to protect itself from harm by the other nation. But if a sudden war erupts everyone will have the capacity to destroy my planet Earth and all of its good things and everything what God made for us on this planet.

The big bang explosion is believed to have happened around 13 billion years back and then it led to the creation of stars around say 400 million years back.

Our world consists of the world of our souls, human body and after death where we may or may not return back to our origins. The soul world is not known to scientists.

I will be disclosing many things, about mankind some known to you, and some not known to anyone on earth, after getting suitable permission from God. Without his permission, I may not have been to allowed to write, about entire mankind, and his existence provided it is not misused.

Most of the things I may have mentioned are already there in history and were borrowed from there and written in books like mine in different ways.

We have three planes on this earth, one is the top layer which is the air around us, another is water, and third is the land plane. All these planes have life organisms.

The air layer has birds as living beings and clouds, the land has animals and human beings and water has fishes, sharks and other type of living organisms.

Birds cannot live on land, except maybe chickens, fish cannot fly or live on land, and neither can humans fly or stay alive in water. All of us are living beings and we cannot stay in the environments of each other.

This is called adaption to the environment we live in. We are adapted to the specific environments and cannot interchange ourselves from one environment to another. The scientists have not been able to explain why human beings cannot live under water or fishes cannot fly or live on land even after so many discoveries.

Science has not actually created anything on its own and these includes medicines. The medicines we see today are already present in plants and we either extract them or make them in chemical plants. In medicine, we identify the molecules present in plants which cure a disease and we reproduce the same molecules in laboratories or factories either by extracting them from plants or making them artificially.

We still cannot make real diamonds, so we cannot make real plants, animals or human beings maybe for the simple reason that every one of them has a soul. I believe every living organism either a plant, animal, human being, fish has a soul. Science does not believe in the existence of a soul but science believes in the existence of software's which run computers, mobile phones and robots.

Without a software no machine would run, neither would robots, mobile phones and some other electronic devices. So how can human beings run without a soul or animals, plants, birds and fishes live without a soul. All the living beings on earth have souls including plants, animals and birds.

There are no guesses right or wrong, and every theory about our origin seems to be correct. whether it is the big bang or our transformation from monkeys to human beings, and us being brought from laboratories on another planet like the test tube babies.

My view of the origin of humans is that we were prepared just like test tube babies in laboratories and I shall discuss this in many chapters of this book, how and when we were created.

Earlier we were not so advanced and development of our minds took long and we were full of superstition and beliefs which made us deny facts which were already known to us.

We all believe in the existence of God and his command over all that is there here and beyond where our naked eyes cannot see. Whatever science may discover and has discovered, it cannot deny that all that is created had a creator.

If there was no creator or God, we would not have churches, temples and mosques. Today our scientific knowledge has increased so we deny the existence of God only because of our scientific achievements but we still cannot create living beings.

A separate subject of biotechnology has also been opened still we are far away from knowing what are biological beings. We are able to create robots and feed them with artificial intelligence. These robots I call them as inorganic human beings as they are made of metal and metal is an inorganic substance.

For any living being to work and think it should be organic which means its body structure should consist of carbon, hydrogen, oxygen, nitrogen and water. The humanoid is entirely made up of organic matter.

Cars, trucks, scooters and bikes were the first robots' we humans created only they could run on wheels just like our horses. These were the first robots although we do not call them the robots in the true sense.

We are also much like those cars and trucks doing the same things again and again. Somebody is an engineer, mechanic, clerk, software engineer and so on each with his own limitations.

Some are all-rounder's not perfect in any one thing. I fit into an all-rounder being a chemical engineer, a software professional, technical writer, author, scientist, philosopher and a lot of things not perfect in any one thing.

When we are perfect in a single thing, we seem to remember many of the details that go with it. If you are a car, you will not behave like a truck as your body is medium and if someone is a heavy body, he is equivalent of a truck and requires heavy work. A software person is soft so he does only programming and can be called lazy who wants less physical work but more something like sitting and doing things.

When I do software work, or write articles and books, I have to convert my body to that behavior which is not easy. My body or my mind refuses to change from car to a truck or to a bike. Once, I start writing, I cannot do programming and if I am moving around doing audits, I cannot sit and do computer work.

That is why people do specific work and to change my work, my mind opposes the switch over and it pains if I try to change my behavior from behaving as a author to behaving as a scientist or a software engineer.

The reason I had to study all software languages, all human history, all human subjects, deep space, aliens and other subjects including medicine and law is not known to me and I tried hard to figure it out and it failed me for reasons unknown. Even after reading entire libraries.

I have not been able to figure out many of the things like human history. I always wonder why we have human history and no animal history except those of dinosaurs' and why the topic of a dinosaur is so interesting to most of the human beings.

But one thing I know is if dinosaurs will exist, we will not exist and if elephants are too many then most other animals will not exist.

Whenever I read things like history, geography, science, space, medicine, nursing, law, software languages and novels, comics, stories and everything that goes with it, I have always wondered where it goes.

I always think why my brain has so much capacity to read and write. Earlier, I read entire libraries and when I wanted to write, it was difficult, and so was reading when I started. I could write only a few words then it came to pages and then articles and books. But it was too difficult to write and today also it is difficult.

I felt I knew so much, and wanted to share it with all of you but when it came to writing them, my brain opposed. It took me a long time to write what I knew or had already been written. For me reading was easy from childhood and I read with speed as fast as I could.

What has reading and writing to do with mankind, nothing at all. But you would not be a doctor, engineer, scientist to any other self, without the skills of reading and writing, and that is what makes us different from animals.

The only thing I cannot see is illusions, or see things beyond our existence, and I can only feel those things that is why I am a human being just like you. I always wonder why I read so much and got to know everything about our planet, but got no answers.

After learning to read and write, scientists created subjects other than history and literature which included science and mathematics. The only subjects people knew earlier was music, history, pottery and utensils making and literature which later expanded into traditional medicine and technological development of making bullock carts and horse carts and drawing water from wells using wooden wheels.

Horse carts and bullock carts were our cars and trucks for those days. Now these have been replaced with advanced vehicles and upgraded using new technology.

I am no Carl Sagan, or Stephen Hawking, but when my knowledge was small, I saw and read all they and other scientists knew combined.

I thought like them, like Edison, Tesla, Einstein, and even read about each and every development that mankind made, and all of the scientists put together. But I am not going to become one like them, as I am a author not a scientist. Though I know all about science and technology, I was never a specialist on those subjects.

My problem is I think very fast, so I am not able to implement things in the speed of thought, so I can only write. It was a compulsion to read about everyone including Jesus, Ram, Prophet Muhammad and everyone, a force so powerful, which made me read everything which I could not oppose.

I cannot make helicopters, and aircrafts or spacecrafts, as I think very fast. I make websites once in a while, but cannot make big ones as I want to do things fast and quickly. These things are not possible practically as computers, are not fast enough, and there are limitations of memory and internet speeds and so on.

Speed is a problem, and if you speed very fast, there are chances of accidents and physical harms and neither the human body, neither our minds can run really fast, as we have resistance in our minds, as well there is resistance from other vehicles who are moving slowly on the roads, which we call traffic.

By giving this example, I want to say not all human minds are the same. Albert Einstein cannot be Thomas Edison. Neither can Carl Sagan be compared to Stephen Hawking.

I am writing all I know, as much as possible in a simple, easy to understand compilation as much as possible. Because, I think very fast, I have accidents in my brain which prevent me from implementing my ideas as a scientist. So, I have incorporated a resistance in my mind to slow down my thinking so it is more practical to the speed of minds on earth.

All I want to write is all in my mind, but it does not match the speed in which i can write everything in one go and have to stop and write every few days, sometimes continues and sometimes as time permits me to be free from my other duties.

I am sure with this book, I will be able to give you all a fair idea of our planet, solar system, the universe, God, mankind and everything is or there will ever be or ever exist anywhere.

I was also forced by unknown spiritual powers, to read all the religious books, that have existed over several thousands of years including all scientific information and discovering and how planets work. These powers exist in oblivion, are invisible to our eyes and run and maintain our planet and protect it from destruction.

Without the existence of these spiritual powers or angels, we would have destroyed ourselves like the empty planet of Mars which we shall study in the later parts of our book. As far as I know, these spiritual powers or angels make rain and run our natural environment system and challenging them would mean we would become simply robots like the ones we are making. These spiritual powers have given us a lot of freedom to think on our own.

As science has advanced, scientists feel the need to do away with religion and religious books and if we do this, we will lose the only contact we have with God. The reason God allows the scientist to exist is that now science develops under protection of big governments and is not dependent on elections. Technology is not decided by politicians but by governments who exist even when there is no elections or mandate by the people.

When a new leader is elected, he is powerful only in front of the people, but the scientists are not at his decision until there is substantial opposition from the public to end those experiments on human beings.

When human beings were made, they were not harmed and God did not do practical experiments on human beings and human embryos.

Are we alone in the Universe

This is how God does experiments on human beings and other animals. He issues guide books or religious texts for them to be moral and honest in society.

If God he sees humans' beings suffer from illnesses, he makes plants which give those medicines, without you or me coming to work in huge factories to make those medicines and buying them for astronomical costs. The factories of God work on their own and do not charge electricity, taxes, or employ laborers for work.

The only thing God asks is to fetch those medicines by picking them from plants, and even those medicines can be dried and transported and kept for a long time if they remain dry and do not catch moisture.

That is the difference between the science of God and our science. God has outlined which food to eat and has made different foods to eat based on the environment in those places.

The environment on all places of the planet cannot be the same. This has been scientifically proved that based on our rotation around the sun, the environment works.

We have already reproduced more than we should and already there is shortage of food and other necessary things like housing and shelter. By cloning we agree to create zombies.

Now many movies have been produced on zombies who are creatures who do not have a mind or a soul. These zombies feed on humans and are barbaric. These zombies are human clones made in laboratories by scientists who want to do something unique like impersonating God.

Some scientist dreams very big and some of them want to make time machines, some want to make cloned humans, go into the deep ends of space and so on. But had we reproduced sensibly, we would have had enough food, housing and shelter for all human beings.

We collect so many taxes, but none of the taxes guarantee food for everyone and that also is left to charity either by us or by charitable organizations. While most of the government expenses go into maintaining armies, space research, nuclear weapons, government staff and security, they leave it on the people to feed themselves and the beggars on the roads.

The beggars are also the result of the same reproduction like the entire mankind. While we are worried about our ever-increasing population, we are not worried about who will feed the beggars. We want to look for more planets same like ours so if there is a population boom, where do we go and live.

Actually, there is no population boom in the first sense. India and China are the only most populated countries on planet Earth. They employ the most people in the armies, government, security and other such things and have put a huge burden on the world.

While China is better off as it has three times more area than India. China has 9.5 million square kilometers of land while India has only 3.28 million square kilometers. So based on the area China has population of only 400 million while India has three times the population in the same area around 1.2 billion. The United States and Europe also have more land and less density of population so there is no need of going to Mars for them to live.

Indians and Chinese along with Bangladesh are the most people on the planet Earth. If we are ever going to Mars, definitely it is not for living over there at least not for the Americans or Europeans or Russians as even Russia has more land than everyone else.

The human body has two types of memories, a short-term memory and a long-term memory. While scientists dispute the existence of God, we know that without creating anything a thing does not come into existence until it is made somewhere.

For example, earthen pots, bridges, roads, bullock carts, airplanes, mobile phones were all created so did millions of things which we call invention.

Electricity, light bulbs, electric motors, cars and other things did not come alive like the Darwin theory or the big bang theory.

The big bang theory tells us that the Universe was created due to a big bang. But then inventions would not have exited and whatever we invented was already present in the universe.

Electricity was present in the universe and we only invented to harness it. Humans have not been able to convert their bodies into anything superior from times memorial and have the same diseases and illnesses. In fact, the number of illnesses has increased so have the medicines to combat the newer diseases.

Based on the Darwin theory of evolution or the theory on big bang, human or animal bodies have not improved in dealing with hot or cold environments and things are pretty much the same.

Only robots and other mechanical equipments can survive harsh weather and we cannot travel in space without a spacesuit.

Even aliens moving around our planet as well as moving in space say they know everything but till date they also have not seen God. So even aliens believe in God even after their advancement sin technology are much ahead of us. Alien bodies are also having the same diseases and illnesses we face even after so much advancement in their science.

No matter how infinite the knowledge we gain it is still a small drop in the ocean of knowledge God has. I have studied many subjects on Earth like history, geography, mathematics, chemical, mechanical, civil engineering. Many types of software's from the basic ones to advanced software's but still have to read a lot to update myself.

Even after studying so much and reading entire libraries in my childhood, I was never perfect and never got to be a genius. I read all the comics and novels available and all stories from around the world. I hardly remember even fifty percent of what I have read till date. Still my knowledge did not become infinite neither there was any improvements in my body or mind.

I have remained the same ordinary person even after reading so much.

Everything we create is finite, has some base of physics, chemistry, science or something in existence or which is present already in the environment.

119 Are we alone in the Universe

We still do not know how clouds move although we think we know, do we know how plants come out of the soil using only seeds, how water manages to reach almost all parts of the planet we call earth or all animals who come alive without using any software program on their own.

No animal is similar but plants are called similar as they look the same to us. All red rose plants are same to us, so are all grape plants of a particular variety.

I believe that God has sent us here to Earth for a purpose which we have to fulfill. We should spread our knowledge for the better of mankind and God has given us unlimited knowledge or the power to think beyond the infinite. While humans are able to think to the finite thoughts and beliefs some of them have indeed reached the infinite thinking of existence. Some of us operate both in the finite and infinite elements of existence as well as the existence of elements beyond infinity.

I too am a human being like the rest of us with my own flesh and blood and all the organs that go along with it and my bone structure and my thinking is no different or unique from others and I don't know magic.

We should believe in a just mankind, spreading happiness, food for all, justice for all and a world in which everyone can live happily with little or no needs.

Most of these things are necessary for a just and a peaceful world. We even after so many thousands of years do not know who we are and our purpose of coming and living on Earth and then going away.

We have not still been able to find out about planets and stars. Even with our vast technological and spiritual developments where we had many spiritual gurus as well as advanced fighter jets and spacecrafts our travel of the space is limits.

Knowledge hides itself behind huge libraries of pure thinking and consciousness and I have read only a little.

Made in the USA
Columbia, SC
01 October 2022